KU-218-810
Christmas Morning
and other Christmas Stories
Miles Kelly

First published in 2015 by Miles Kelly Publishing Ltd
Harding's Barn, Bardfield End Green, Thaxted, Essex, CM6 3PX, UK

This edition printed 2018

2 4 6 8 10 9 7 5 3

Publishing Director Belinda Gallagher
Creative Director Jo Cowan
Editorial Director Rosie Neave
Senior Editor Sarah Parkin
Design Manager Joe Jones
Production Elizabeth Collins, Jennifer Brunwin-Jones
Reprographics Stephan Davis, Jennifer Cozens
Assets Lorraine King

ISBN 978-1-78209-831-7

Printed in China

British Library Cataloguing-in-Publication Data
A catalogue record for this book is available from the British Library

ACKNOWLEDGEMENTS
The publishers would like to thank the following artists who have contributed to this book:

Front cover: Simona Sanfilippo (Plum Pudding Illustration Agency)

Inside illustrations:
Decorative frame Rachel Cloyne (Pickled Ink)
The Josephs' Christmas Charlotte Cooke (The Bright Agency)
Christmas Morning Antonia Woodward (Plum Pudding Illustration Agency)
The Cratchits' Christmas Goose Natalia Moore (Advocate Art)
Thank You Letters Simona Sanfilippo (Plum Pudding Illustration Agency)

Made with paper from a sustainable forest

www.mileskelly.net

Contents

The Josephs' Christmas 4
Christmas Morning 14
The Cratchits' Christmas Goose 20
Thank You Letters 32

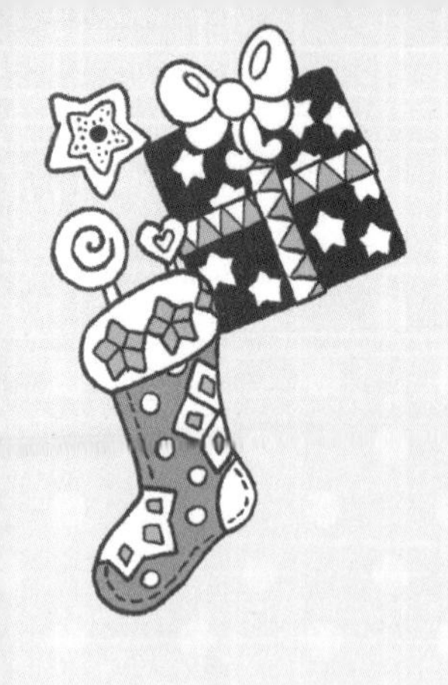

The Josephs' Christmas

By L M Montgomery

The month before Christmas was always the most exciting and mysterious time in the Joseph household. Such scheming and planning, such counting of small hoards, and such hiding and smuggling of things out of sight, as went on among the little Josephs!

During this particular December the planning and contriving had been more

difficult and the results less satisfactory than usual. The Josephs were poor at any time, but this winter they were poorer than ever. But on Christmas Eve every little Joseph went to bed with a clear conscience, for was there not on the corner table in the kitchen a small mountain of tiny – sometimes very tiny – gifts labelled with the names of recipients and givers?

It was beginning to snow when the small, small Josephs went to bed, and when the big, small Josephs climbed the stairs it was snowing thickly.

Mr and Mrs Joseph sat down before the fire and listened to the wind howling about the house.

"I'm glad I'm not driving over the prairie tonight," said Mr Joseph. "It's quite a storm.

Mary, this is the first Christmas since we came west that we couldn't afford some little extras for them, even if it was only a box of nuts and candy."

Mrs Joseph sighed over Jimmy's worn jacket that she was mending, but then she smiled at Mr Joseph.

"Never mind, John," she said. "Things will be better next Christmas, we'll hope. We've got each other, and good health and spirits, and a Christmas wouldn't be much without those if we had all the presents in the world."

Mr Joseph nodded.

"That's so. I don't want to grumble, but I did want to get Maggie a 'real live doll', as she calls it. There was one at Fisher's store today – a big beauty with real hair, and eyes that opened and shut. Just fancy Maggie's

face if she saw that tomorrow morning."

"Don't let's fancy it," said Mrs Joseph. "That can't be someone at the door!"

"It is, though," said Mr Joseph as he strode to the door and flung it open.

Two snowed-up figures were standing on the porch. As they stepped in, the Josephs recognized one of them as Mr Ralston, a wealthy merchant in a small town fifteen miles away.

"Late hour for callers, isn't it?" said Mr Ralston. "The fact is, our horse has about given out, and the storm is so bad that we can't proceed. This is my wife, and we are on our way to spend Christmas with my brother's family at Lindsay. Can you take us in for the night, Mr Joseph?"

"Certainly, and welcome!" exclaimed Mr Joseph heartily. "I'll see to putting your

horse away now, Mr Ralston. This way, if you please."

When the two men came into the house again, Mrs Ralston and Mrs Joseph were sitting at the fire. Mr Ralston put the big basket he was carrying down on a bench in the corner.

"Thought I'd better bring our Christmas flummery in," he said. "You see, Mrs Joseph, my brother has a big family, so we are taking them a lot of Santa Claus stuff. Mrs Ralston packed this basket, and goodness knows what she put in it, but she half cleaned out my store."

Mrs Joseph gave a little sigh in spite of herself, and looked wistfully at the heap of gifts on the corner table.

Mrs Ralston looked too. "Santa Claus seems to have visited you already," she said.

The Josephs laughed.

"Our Santa Claus is somewhat out of pocket this year," said Mr Joseph frankly.

A shakedown was spread in the kitchen for the unexpected guests, and presently the Ralstons found themselves alone. Mrs Ralston went over to the Christmas table and looked at the little gifts half tenderly and half pityingly.

"They're not much like the contents of our basket, are they?" she said, as she touched the calendar Jimmie had made for Mollie out of cardboard and autumn leaves and grasses.

"Just what I was thinking," returned her husband, "and I was thinking of something else, too. I've a notion that I'd like to see some of the things in our basket right here on this table."

"I'd like to see them all on this table," said Mrs Ralston promptly. "Let's just leave them here, Edward. Roger's family will have plenty of presents without them, and for that matter we can send them ours when we go back home."

"Just as you say," agreed Mr Ralston. "I very much like the idea of giving the small folk of this household a rousing good Christmas for once."

Then by comparing the names attached to the gifts on the table they managed to divide theirs up pretty evenly among the little Josephs.

When all was done Mrs Ralston said, "We will be going before daylight, probably, and in the hurry of getting off I hope that Mr and Mrs Joseph will not notice the difference till we're gone."

It worked out as she had planned. Breakfast for the travellers was cooked and eaten by lamplight, then the horse and sleigh were brought to the door and Mr Ralston carried out his empty basket.

"Goodbye and a merry Christmas to you all," he said.

Mrs Joseph went back to the kitchen and her eyes fell on the table in the corner.

"Why—!" Mrs Joseph said, and snatched off the cover.

Mr Joseph came too, and looked and whistled in shock.

There really seemed to be everything on the table that the hearts of children could desire – three pairs of skates, a fur cap, gleaming new books, a writing desk, a pair of fur-topped gloves, and also a china cup and saucer.

All these were to be seen at the first glance, and in one corner of the table was a big box filled with candies and nuts and raisins, and in the other, a doll with curling golden hair and brown eyes, dressed in real clothes and with all her wardrobe in a trunk beside her. Pinned to her dress was a note with Maggie's name written on it.

"The children will go wild with delight," said Mrs Joseph happily.

They very nearly did when they all came scrambling down the stairs a little later.

Such a Christmas had never been known

in the Joseph household before. Maggie clasped her doll with shining eyes. And as for the big box of good things, why, everybody appreciated that.

I'm glad to be able to say, too, that the little Josephs did not forget to appreciate the gifts they had prepared for each other. Mollie thought her calendar just too pretty for anything, and Jimmie was sure the new mittens that Maggie had knitted for him were the nicest mittens ever worn.

Christmas Morning

An extract from *Peter and Polly in Winter*
by Rose Lucia

Early Christmas morning Peter awoke. He heard a noise in Mother's room, so he knew that he might get up.

He pushed open the door. "Merry Christmas! Merry Christmas!" he shouted.

"Merry Christmas," said Mother, hugging him tightly.

"Merry Christmas," said Father, tossing him up into the air. "Did you see Santa Claus last night?"

Just then Polly ran in. "Oh, oh, it is Christmas!" she cried. "Merry Christmas! Merry Christmas! Just see what I found in my bed."

It was a box of animal crackers. They were all sheep.

"Oh Father! You did it for a joke. You know I do not like mutton."

There were to be no more presents until after breakfast, so the children dressed quickly. It was very hard for them to eat anything at all.

At last Polly said, "I cannot wait another second. I will eat my breakfast with my dinner. Here comes Grandmother. Now may we open the door and see the tree?"

"In just a minute," said Father. "You say 'Merry Christmas' to Grandmother. I have one last thing for the tree. You may come in

when I call." And out he ran.

"I wonder what it is," said Polly, excitedly. "I can hear him coming back through the side door."

Then Grandmother came in, and Polly forgot to wonder any more.

At last they heard Father shout, "Come!"

Polly opened the door, and the children rushed in.

"Oh! Oh!" said Polly.

"Oh! Oh!" said Peter.

Such a beautiful tree they had never before seen. It was hung with strings of popped corn and red cranberries. It was covered with coloured balls and big gold stars. Over it was white, shiny stuff that looked like snow.

It had candy bags and oranges. At the top, there was a doll with wings. And there

were many boxes and packages.

"Oh! Oh! Oh!" said both children again.

"Do you like it?" asked Mother.

"I never saw anything so pretty," said Polly. "Is that a fairy at the top?"

"I think it is Santa Claus' little girl," said Peter. "I should very much like to have her for my own."

"Should you rather have that than anything else here?" asked Father.

"I think so, Father. May I?"

"Walk around the tree and see if you are sure, my son."

Peter did as he was told. He had not taken many steps when he jumped back with a cry.

"What is it? What is it?" he asked.

Polly ran forwards, and what do you think she saw?

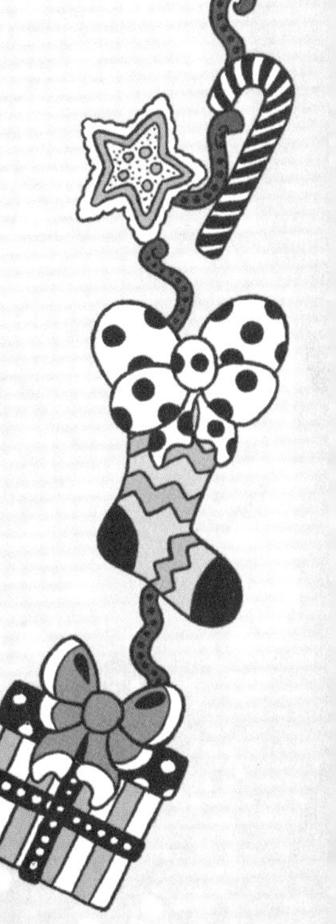

On the other side of the tree something moved. Polly saw two large eyes, two long ears, a brown head, and then she knew that it was a pony.

"Peter, Peter!" she cried, "here is the pony! It is by the Christmas tree!"

"Lead her out," said Father. "Her name is Brownie. She is Grandmother's present to you both. She is half yours and half Peter's."

"Oh, Grandmother!" cried Polly. "I thank you now, but I will thank you even better before long."

"Which half is mine, Grandmother?" asked Peter.

"Half of both halves," Grandmother replied. "Why?"

"Nothing," said Peter. "I love both her halves. And I love you, too. And I love the tree, and Christmas, and everybody."

"And so you should," said Father. "Come now, we will take Brownie to her stable. Then you may get the presents off the tree."

The Cratchits' Christmas Goose

An extract from *A Christmas Carol*
by Charles Dickens

The Cratchit family are a poor family living in Victorian London. Martha works away from home, and only gets one day off. The Cratchits have no oven, so their goose is cooked at the bakers and then brought home, and they boil their pudding in the large copper bowl, which they usually use for washing their clothes.

"What has ever got your precious father then?" said Mrs Cratchit. "And your brother, Tiny Tim! And Martha! She wasn't as late last Christmas

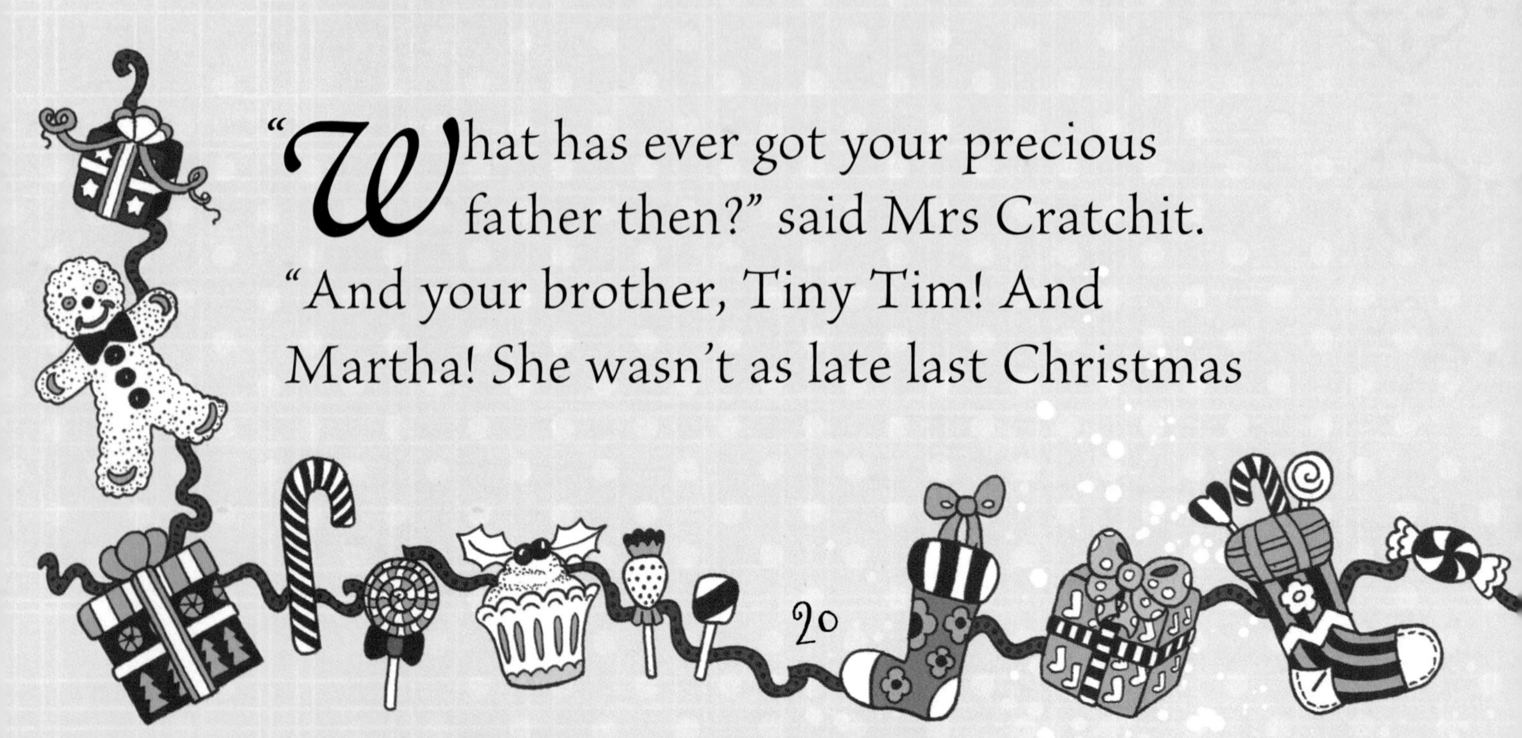

Day by half an hour!"

"Here's Martha, Mother!" said a girl, appearing as she spoke.

"Here's Martha, Mother!" cried the two young Cratchits. "Hurrah! There's such a goose, Martha!"

"Why, bless your heart alive, my dear, how late you are!" said Mrs Cratchit, kissing her a dozen times, and taking off her shawl and bonnet for her.

"We'd a deal of work to finish up last night," replied the girl, "and had to clear away this morning, Mother!"

"Never mind so long as you are come," said Mrs Cratchit. "Sit ye down before the fire and have a warm, Lord bless ye!"

"No, no! There's Father coming," cried the two young Cratchits, who were everywhere at once. "Hide, Martha, hide!"

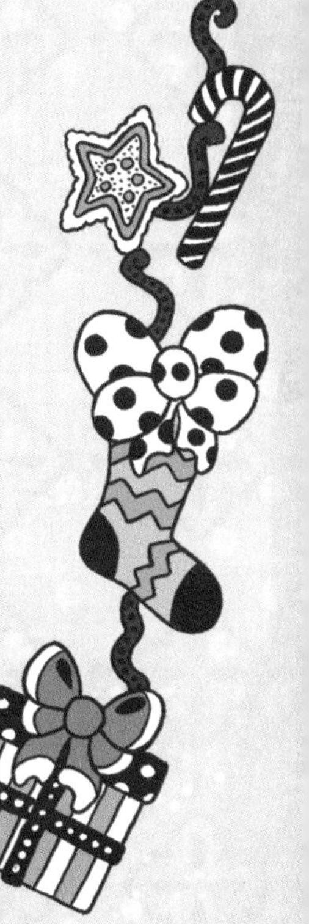

So Martha hid herself, and in came little Bob, the father, with at least three feet of comforter hanging down before him, and his threadbare clothes darned up and brushed to look seasonable, and Tiny Tim upon his shoulder. Alas for Tiny Tim, he bore a little crutch, and had his limbs supported by an iron frame.

"Why, where's our Martha?" cried Bob Cratchit, looking round.

"Not coming," said Mrs Cratchit.

"Not coming!" said Bob. "Not coming upon Christmas Day!"

Martha didn't like to see him disappointed, even if it were only in joke, so she came out from behind the closet door, and ran into his arms. The two young Cratchits hustled Tiny Tim, and bore him off into the wash house, that he might hear

the pudding singing in the copper.

"And how did little Tim behave?" asked Mrs Cratchit, when she had rallied Bob on his credulity and Bob had hugged his daughter to his heart's content.

"As good as gold," said Bob, "and better."

His little crutch was heard on the floor, and back came Tiny Tim before another word was spoken, escorted by his brother and sister to his stool before the fire.

And while Bob, turning up his cuffs, compounded some hot mixture in a jug with lemons, and stirred it round and round, and put it on the hob to simmer, Master Peter and the two young Cratchits went to fetch the goose, with which they soon returned in high procession.

You might have thought a goose the rarest of all birds, and in truth, it was

something like it in that house.

Mrs Cratchit made the gravy (ready beforehand in a little saucepan) hissing hot, Master Peter mashed

the potatoes with incredible vigour, Miss Belinda sweetened up the apple sauce, and Martha dusted the hot plates.

Bob took Tiny Tim beside him in a tiny corner, at the table. The two young Cratchits set chairs for everybody, not forgetting themselves, and mounting guard upon their posts, crammed spoons into their mouths, lest they should shriek for goose before their turn came to be helped.

At last the dishes were set on the table and grace was said. It was succeeded by a breathless pause, as Mrs Cratchit, looking slowly all along the carving knife, prepared to plunge it in the breast. But when she did, and when the long-expected gush of stuffing issued forth, one murmur of delight arose all around the table, and even Tiny Tim, excited by the two young Cratchits, beat on

the table with the handle of his knife, and cried hurrah!

There never was such a goose. Bob said he didn't believe there ever was such a goose cooked. Its tenderness and flavour, size and cheapness, were the themes of universal admiration.

Eked out by the apple sauce and mashed potatoes, it was a sufficient dinner for the whole family. Indeed, as Mrs Cratchit said with great delight (surveying one small atom of a bone on the dish), they hadn't eaten it all at last! Yet everyone had had enough, and the youngest Cratchits in particular were steeped in sage and onion to the eyebrows!

But now, the plates being changed by Miss Belinda, Mrs Cratchit left the room alone – too nervous to bear witnesses – to

take the pudding up and bring it in.

Suppose it should not be done enough? Suppose it should break in turning out? Suppose somebody should have got over the wall of the backyard and stolen the pudding, while they were merry with the goose? All sorts of horrors were supposed.

Hallo! A great deal of steam! The pudding was out of the copper. A smell like a washing day! That was the cloth. A smell like an eating house and a pastry cook's next door to each other, with a laundress next door to that! That was the pudding.

In half a minute Mrs Cratchit

entered, flushed, but smiling proudly, carrying the pudding, which looked like a speckled cannonball, so hard and firm, blazing in half of half-a-quartern of ignited brandy, and with Christmas holly stuck into the top.

Oh, a wonderful pudding! Bob Cratchit said, and calmly too, that he regarded it as the greatest success Mrs Cratchit had achieved since their marriage. Mrs Cratchit said that now the weight was off her mind, she would confess she had had her doubts about the quantity of flour.

Everybody had something to say about it, but nobody said or thought it was at all a small pudding for so large a family. It would have been flat heresy to do so. And any Cratchit would have blushed to hint at such a thing.

At last the dinner was all done, the cloth was cleared, the hearth swept, and the fire made up.

The compound in the jug being tasted and considered perfect, apples and oranges were put upon the table, and a shovelful of chestnuts on the fire.

Then all the Cratchit family drew round the hearth, in what Bob Cratchit called a circle, meaning half a one. And at Bob Cratchit's elbow stood the family display of glass – two tumblers, and a custard-cup without a handle.

These held the hot stuff from the jug, however, as well as golden goblets would have done, and Bob served it out with beaming looks, while the chestnuts on the fire sputtered and cracked noisily.

Then Bob proposed, "A Merry

Christmas to us all, my dears. God bless us!"

Which all the family re-echoed.

"God bless us every one!" said Tiny Tim, the last of all.

Thank You Letters

An extract from *Betty Trevor*
by Mrs G De Horne Vaizey

Betty and Jill (whose full name is Margaret) are sisters. A sovereign was a gold coin, and a crown was a silver one, both worth quite a generous amount of money when this story was written.

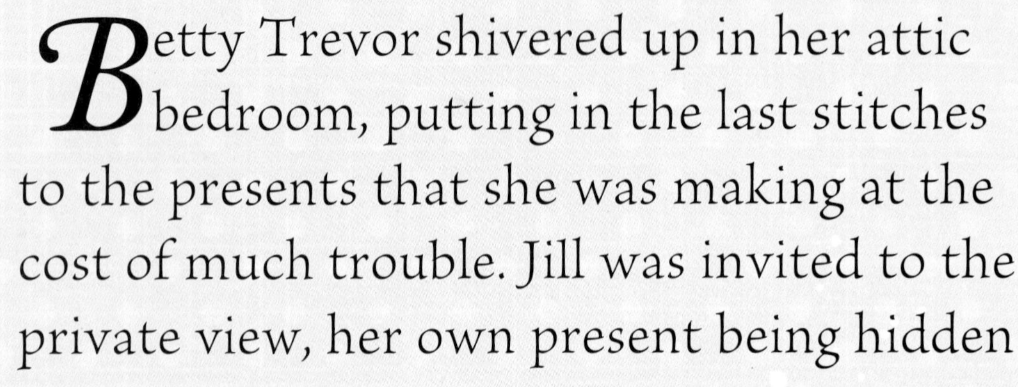

Betty Trevor shivered up in her attic bedroom, putting in the last stitches to the presents that she was making at the cost of much trouble. Jill was invited to the private view, her own present being hidden

away, and expressed admiration.

"Such a lot of work though!" she declared. "Look at me, I've done the whole thing in one afternoon! Sailed out with my savings in my purse – and I got fifteen really handsome presents."

"Jill, you haven't! It isn't possible!"

"It is. It only needs management. I've kept all the chocolate boxes we have had given to us during the year – six of them – and they look wonderful filled with sweets at sixpence a pound. I collected mother's old scent bottles too, and bought a shilling's worth of eau de Cologne to fill them. Such a joke! It didn't quite go round, so I put some water in the last, and it's turned quite milky. I'll have to give that to Pam. She'll think it something new and superior. I've got sticking-plaster for the boys – they are

sure to cut their fingers some day – and a beautiful needle book for Mother."

She skipped downstairs and, sitting down in the drawing room, proceeded to write a number of letters, in which words and spaces were curiously mingled.

Dear Aunt Margaret, thank you so much for the beautiful... It is just what I wanted. It was so nice of you to send it to me. I think it is... I hope you are quite well, and not having asthma any more... Your loving niece, Margaret.

Darling Cousin Flo, I am so awfully obliged to you for the lovely... It is just what I wanted. I am so pleased to have it. It will just do for...

I think Christmas is ripping, don't you? Please write soon.

Dear Mrs Gregory, it is most kind of you to remember me with such a nice present. The... is just what I wanted. I am much obliged to you for remembering me. Has not Christmas Day been... this year? I am your loving little friend, Margaret Meredith Trevor.

My own dear, darling Norah, what an angel you are to send me that perfectly lovely... It is just exactly what I wanted, and I am so proud to have it. Come round tomorrow and see my things. I've got... altogether. Isn't that a lot? Don't you call this weather...? Your own Jill.

She was scribbling away when a hand fell on her shoulder and a voice cried, "Eh,

what? Too busy to hear me come in, were you? What's the meaning of this?"

Starting up, she saw General Digby bending over her. This was not the first visit which the General had paid. He was a lonely old man, and to spend a few minutes in the cheery atmosphere of a family made a nice break for him.

"Writing Christmas letters, eh?" boomed the General loudly. "Sending off your presents, I suppose. What? Thanking people for presents, do you say? That's a bit previous, isn't it? What's the hurry?"

"There's always so much going on after Christmas, when the boys are at home, and it's such a bore

being in the house writing letters. I use up the odd times before in getting them as ready as I can, and then it only takes a minute to fill in the spaces."

She held out a specimen letter and General Digby went off into a convulsion of laughter, coughing and panting for breath.

Jill pounded him on the back until he recovered himself enough to shake her off, declaring that the cure was worse than the disease. He sank into a chair and wiped his eyes with a handkerchief.

"Where's my letter?" he inquired. "I suppose there's one addressed to me among all that number. Was I as fortunate as the rest in sending

just what was wanted? You are a young woman of a great many wants, it seems to me. Tell you what now – fill up the blanks, and I'll see if I can come up to expectation!"

"Oh no!" cried Jill, blushing with embarrassment. "There is no letter for you. I truly never thought you would give us anything. I couldn't possibly choose myself. It's awfully good of you to think of it, but, really, anything. It's like this, you see – I want anything I can get!"

"Oh, you do, do you?" cried the General. "Nothing like honesty in this world, my dear. Well, we must see what we can do! I'll bend my mind to the question, and you shall know the result on Christmas Day."

The Trevors' programme on Christmas Day differed from those of their friends. No presents were given in the morning. It

was enough excitement to know that it was Christmas Day, and to linger over a late and luxurious breakfast before going to church. On their return, the sight of the hall table banished every other thought, for on it lay a pile of Christmas cards. Betty pounced on them and gave a shout of delight.

"There's money inside! There is, I can feel it. Mine's quite small – like a – a—"

She opened her own in a flutter of excitement. Inside there was a folded piece of paper enclosing a second envelope. In her haste Betty ripped it open, and held up to view a brand new sovereign.

"It is! How simply lovely! I was so hard up – and now! Who can have sent it?"

She picked up the piece of paper which

she had dropped in her haste, and read, "With the best wishes of General Digby."

Jack and Jill had each a new ten-shilling piece, and Pam a magnificent silver crown.

"He said he would send me something, but I never thought it would be money. It's what I like better than anything else, to be rich in the Christmas holidays!" Jill cried.

Mrs Trevor smiled and said, "So he seemed to think. He asked my permission before sending his presents in this form, and said he would like to give you money, because when he was a boy an old lady used to send new coins to himself and his brothers every Christmas, and he had never forgotten the pleasure they gave him."